Amazing Dinosaurs

The Fastest, the Smallest, the Fiercest, and the Tallest

Cover illustration by Richard Walz

A GOLDEN BOOK • NEW YORK

Western Publishing Company, Inc., Racine, Wisconsin 53404

© 1991 Western Publishing Company, Inc. DINOSAURS © 1987 Mary Elting. Illustrations © 1987 Gabriele Nenzioni and Mauro Cutrona. TINY DINOSAURS © 1988 Steven Lindblom. Illustrations © 1988 Gino D'Achille. FLYING DINOSAURS © 1990 Steven Lindblom. Illustrations © 1990 Christopher Santoro. All rights reserved. Printed in the U.S.A. No part of this book may be reproduced or copied in any form without written permission from the publisher. All trademarks are the property of Western Publishing Company, Inc. Library of Congress Catalog Card Number: 90-84656 ISBN: 0-307-15747-4/ISBN: 0-307-65747-7 (lib. bdg.)   A MCMXCI

Dinosaurs

The first dinosaurs that we know about lived almost 225 million years ago. The last ones died about 65 million years ago.

Dinosaur means "terrible lizard," and many of them *were* ferocious meat-eaters. They belonged to a group called theropods (THER-o-pods).

But most dinosaurs ate plants. The biggest of the plant-eaters were the gentle giants called sauropods (SAWR-o-pods). Other plant-eaters included the duck-billed dinosaurs, or hadrosaurs (HAD-row-sawrs); horned dinosaurs, or ceratopsians (sair-uh-TOPS-ee-yans); armored dinosaurs, or ankylosaurs (ang-KILE-o-sawrs) and their relatives the stegosaurs (STEG-o-sawrs); and many more.

Nobody ever saw a live dinosaur. How, then, do we know they were real? Their bones tell us. When a dinosaur died, mud and blowing sand often covered its body. Its flesh decayed, and after a long time, the buried bones became as hard as stone. These stony pieces of dinosaurs are called fossils. Buried dinosaur eggs and even dinosaur footprints made in mud or sand became fossils, too.

Sometimes the people who hunt for dinosaur bones find a whole skeleton with all the bones joined together. But usually the bones are all mixed up. Then someone has to figure out how to put the skeleton together. That isn't always easy.

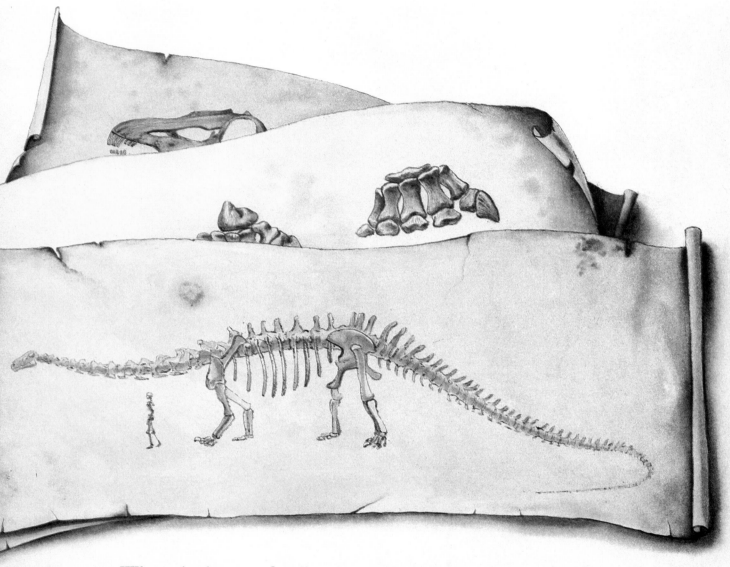

When the bones of a dinosaur called Diplodocus (dih-PLOD-o-kus) were discovered, some people thought they belonged to a giant creeping lizard. Yet scientists kept studying the bones. Finally they could tell how Diplodocus really looked when it was alive.

Diplodocus and its cousin Apatosaurus (a-pat-o-SAWR-us) belonged to the group of dinosaurs that had very long necks. They were called sauropods. From the top of its head to the tip of its tail, Diplodocus was about 90 feet long. That is almost as long as three school buses. Diplodocus had the longest of all dinosaur tails.

Diplodocus

Diplodocus and the other sauropods had very small brains. Did this mean that they were stupid? People used to think so. But now scientists say that sauropods were smart enough to get along very well in the world as it was millions of years ago.

Apatosaurus may have had a shorter tail than Diplodocus, but its body was twice as heavy. In fact, Apatosaurus used to be called Brontosaurus (bron-tow-SAWR-us), which means "thunder lizard," because of the noise its heavy feet must have made when it walked.

Apatosaurus

The skeleton of a sauropod called Brachiosaurus (brack-ee-o-SAWR-us) was 80 feet long and so tall it could have rested its chin on the roof of a building four stories high. For a long time people thought it was the biggest dinosaur in the world.

Then Dr. James Jensen discovered bones that belonged to an even taller sauropod. He called it Ultrasaurus (ul-tra-SAWR-us). It could have looked you in the eye if you were in a seat at the top of a Ferris wheel 60 feet high. Ultrasaurus probably weighed as much as 20 elephants.

Brachiosaurus

Scientists hope to find the bones of an even bigger dinosaur called Breviparopus (brev-ip-a-RO-pus). So far they have discovered only the footprints it left in North Africa. How could fossil footprints tell its size? They are so big and so far apart that only a gigantic animal could have made them. Breviparopus may have been twice as long as Brachiosaurus.

Now look at the fossil dinosaur footprint at the bottom of this page. It is actual size and the smallest one ever found. You could hold in your hand the tiny animal that made it. The birdlike shape of its toes tells scientists that this dinosaur walked on its hind feet.

Procompsognathus (pro-comp-sog-NAY-thus), which was about the size of a turkey, and Segisaurus (see-gih-SAWR-us), which was not much bigger than a goose, also walked on their hind feet.

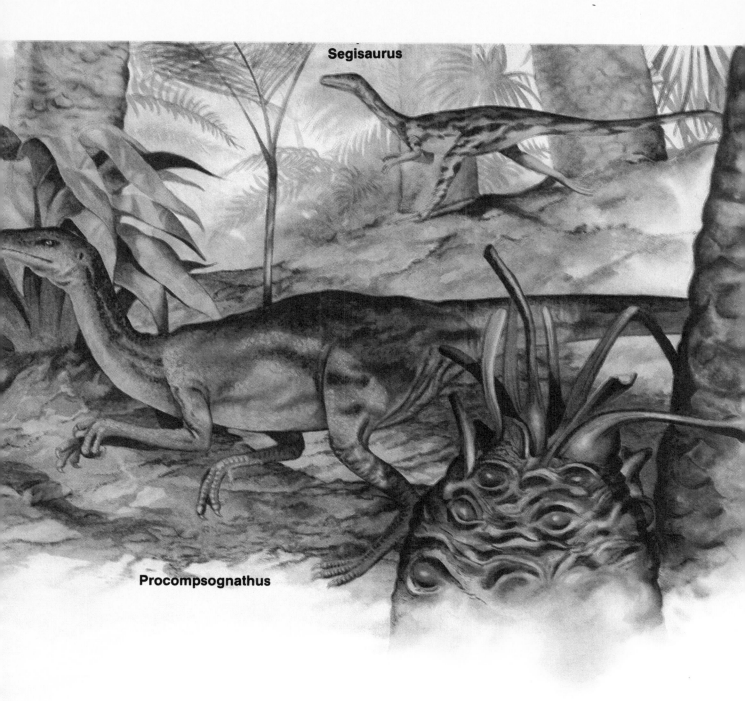

Segisaurus

Procompsognathus

The skeleton of Mussasaurus (muss-uh-SAWR-us) was the tiniest one ever found—only eight inches long. But scientists say it was just a baby dinosaur. How do they know? The bones and joints of a baby animal are not as well developed as those of an adult animal.

You could sit comfortably in the palm of the biggest dinosaur hand ever found. It belonged to giant Deinocheirus (dine-o-KIRE-rus). The scientist who discovered the huge hand bones, arm bones, and claws never located the rest of the body, but she thinks Deinocheirus was a meat-eater. Why? The claws and arms are like those of Megalosaurus and other well-known meat-eaters.

A good way to tell whether a dinosaur was a meat-eater or a plant-eater is to look at its teeth. Plant-eaters had either flat grinding teeth, or teeth cut like scissor blades, and could mash and chop leaves, twigs, and fruit. Dinosaurs with long pointed teeth were meat-eaters called theropods.

Diplodocus

Allosaurus

Tyrannosaurus (tye-ran-o-SAWR-us), one of the fiercest theropods, had teeth like huge daggers. Its jaws could open wide enough to take enormous bites that it swallowed in one gulp. If you could open your jaws the way Tyrannosaurus did, you could get a whole watermelon in your mouth.

Tyrannosaurus

Iguanodon

Deinonychus

Deinonychus (dine-o-NYE-kus) was a small, speedy theropod with a lot of teeth that had jagged edges like steak knives. On the middle toe of each of its hind feet was a claw that could rip through the toughest hide. Whole bands of these ferocious little dinosaurs probably hunted together. When they found a big plant-eater, such as Iguanodon (i-GWAN-o-don), they all leapt on it, biting and slashing with their terrible claws.

Stegosaurus

Stegosaurus (steg-o-SAWR-us) had a strange shape, even for a dinosaur. The triangular plates on its back and neck were made of bone. Grooves in the plates may have held blood vessels, which could have made the plates work like radiators. On a hot day wind blowing over the plates would cool Stegosaurus by carrying heat away from its blood. The plates, along with spikes on Stegosaurus's tail, were probably scary enough to discourage any hungry meat-eater.

Stegosaurus was as big as a garbage truck. Its cousin Lexovisaurus (lex-o-vee-SAWR-us), only half that large, had fewer plates on its back but many more sharp spines. A large spine, pointing downward, grew on each of its sides, just behind its hips. Another cousin, Dacentrurus (duh-sen-TRU-rus), had no plates. Instead, two rows of dangerous-looking spikes stuck out all along its back.

Lexovisaurus

Euoplocephalus

Tyrannosaurus

Ankylosaurs were also relatives of Stegosaurus. They had bony slabs like armor covering much of their bodies. Some ankylosaurs were as big as buses, and the smallest, called Minmi (MIN-mee), was about the size of a bear. It had round chunks of bone under its skin for protection. Spikes on the sides of Edmontonia (ed-mon-TOE-nee-ya) would have made it especially hard to eat. Euoplocephalus (you-op-lo-SEF-uh-lus) had an extra weapon. Its ten-foot-long tail ended in a huge bony knob. With one powerful swing of the tail, Euoplocephalus could break a meat-eater's jaw.

Dinosaurs called hadrosaurs had wide, rounded snouts like duckbills. In fact, "duckbill" is their nickname. Duckbills could probably swim if they had to escape from meat-eating theropods. But they could also travel quickly on dry land. How do we know? Their toes ended in small hooves, which were good for running.

Parasaurolophus

Some duckbills had skull bones with strange tall crests. What were they for? To explain them, scientists thought about the way duckbills lived. Great herds of them stayed together, just as different kinds of African antelope do today. The shape of an antelope's horns seems to help it recognize its own kind if it gets separated from the group. Perhaps the shape of a crest helped a lost duckbill in the same way.

Millions of dinosaurs called ceratopsians ("horned faces") once roamed the Earth. Chasmosaurus (kaz-mo-SAWR-us) and its many ceratopsian cousins carried around large bony slabs called frills that jutted out from the back of their skulls. The frill probably protected their necks. It also supported the enormous muscles that worked their powerful jaws and kept their heavy heads in place.

Torosaurus

Like the other ceratopsians, huge Torosaurus (tor-o-SAWR-us) was a plant-eater. If Torosaurus leaned against a small oak tree, the trunk would snap. Then, with its scissor-like teeth, Torosaurus could chew the whole thing up, leaves, wood, and all.

Triceratops (try-SAIR-uh-tops) had a short frill, but its top horns were more than three feet long. They could have jabbed holes in a meat-eater's stomach. Even Tyrannosaurus probably hesitated to attack it!

Triceratops

Tiny Dinosaurs

The dinosaurs that walked the Earth millions of years ago were the biggest animals that ever lived on land.

Ultrasaurus (ul-tra-SAWR-us) may have been bigger than a five-story building.

Fierce Tyrannosaurus (tye-ran-o-SAWR-us) was as tall as a telephone pole and weighed as much as a schoolbus. When he ran, the ground must have trembled.

Hiding in the bushes as these monsters thundered by were smaller creatures. What were these creatures? Some were lizards, others were small mammals, and others were...

TINY DINOSAURS!

Not all dinosaurs were giants. Dinosaurs came in all sizes, just as animals do today. Many dinosaurs were no bigger than you. Some were even smaller.

Dinosaurs once lived all over the world. Some may have lived right where you live today. But the world did not look like it does now. There were no people, houses, or roads then. Many kinds of strange plants grew everywhere. The weather may have been much warmer than it is now.

Saltopus (sal-TOE-pus) was one of the earliest and tiniest dinosaurs. It lived 160 million years ago. Saltopus was only the size of a cat and ate bugs and lizards. With its long legs it looked like a featherless roadrunner and must have been very fast.

People used to think of dinosaurs as being great big lizards, but we now know that they were not. Lizards are cold-blooded, and today scientists think some dinosaurs may have been warm-blooded. Many dinosaurs walked on their hind legs, like birds. They carried their tails in the air for balance instead of dragging them on the ground. Lizards cannot do those things.

Compsognathus (comp-so-NATH-us) was a very small dinosaur. It had a close cousin, Archaeopteryx (ar-kee-OP-ter-ix). Both had long tails and sharp teeth. Looking at the bones of these two cousins it is very hard to tell them apart.

But Archaeopteryx also had wings and feathers. It was a good flier. It may also have been able to climb trees, using the claws on its wings and legs.

These tiny dinosaurs fed on insects, lizards, and other tiny animals. They were fast and agile. They had to keep out of the way of their hungry bigger cousins.

Being such little animals in a world of giants must have made most of the tiny dinosaurs very timid. They probably lived like mice or chipmunks do today, darting about quietly in search of food.

Not Deinonychus (dine-o-NYE-kus), though. A little smaller than a man, it was one of the fiercest dinosaurs of all. Deinonychus had a mouth full of sharp teeth, and a sharp middle claw on each back foot for slashing. It was very fast and could outrun anything it couldn't eat.

But not all the tiny dinosaurs were meat-eaters. Some ate only plants. Psittacosaurus (sit-a-ko-SAWR-us), or "parrot-lizard," had a powerful beak like a parrot's. It used its beak to eat tough plants and small trees, which it ground up in its stomach with stones it swallowed.

Another plant-eater, Ammosaurus (am-mo-SAWR-us), was only the size of a large dog. Like its big cousin Apatosaurus (a-pat-o-SAWR-us), it spent most of its time on four legs, although it could stand and walk on two.

Heterodontosaurus (het-er-o-don-to-SAWR-us) was only the size of a turkey and fed on plants. With its grinding teeth it could eat almost anything. With its biting teeth it could fight off other dinosaurs.

Another tiny dinosaur, Scutellosaurus (scut-tle-o-SAWR-us), didn't need sharp teeth to protect itself. Its back was covered with bony armor plates. Scutellosaurus had a tail that was twice as long as its body.

Some tiny dinosaurs were tiny because they were babies. Even the biggest of the dinosaurs were tiny when they hatched from eggs. Many dinosaur babies were so small, they would have fit in your hand. Even a newly hatched Apatosaurus was probably smaller than a cat.

You might not recognize a baby Stegosaurus
(steg-o-SAWR-us) unless you saw it with a grown-up one.
Stegosauruses may not have grown their back plates until
they got older.

Maiasaura (mye-a-SAWR-a) was only the size of a robin when it hatched from its egg, but it grew up to be 30 feet long.

How did such big dinosaur mothers ever care for such tiny babies? They must have been very gentle for their size. Scientists used to think that dinosaurs just laid their eggs and left them, the way turtles do today. Now we believe that many dinosaurs fed and cared for their young, the way birds do.

A dinosasur mother was too big to sit on her eggs without breaking them. Instead she covered them with leaves and moss to keep them warm until they hatched. The little dinosaurs would stay close to the nest until they were big enough to go off on their own.

Many dinosaurs lived in herds with other dinosaurs like themselves. There would have been many little dinosaurs in the group at one time. Did they play with each other? Maybe they did, chasing each other and splashing about in the water.

The last dinosaurs died out 65 million years ago. You can never see live dinosaurs—just their bones. But many scientists think today's birds are direct relatives of the dinosaurs. So the next time you feed the birds, you can imagine you are feeding tiny dinosaurs!

Flying Dinosaurs

Millions of years ago, when dinosaurs ruled Earth, pterosaurs (TARE-uh-sawrs) ruled the skies.

Most people think of these creatures as flying dinosaurs, but they were really only cousins of the dinosaurs. Pterosaurs and dinosaurs probably evolved from the same early reptiles, called thecodonts (THEEK-uh-donts).

The first pterosaur to be discovered and named by
scientists was Pterodactylus (tare-uh-DAK-til-us).
Pterodactylus was the size of a hawk and had a long beak.
It may have lived on the mud flats and searched the mud
at low tide for sea worms to eat.

Pterosaur means winged reptile. When the first pterosaur fossils were found 200 years ago, scientists thought pterosaurs must have been reptiles. Their heads and teeth were like those of alligators. But even though pterosaurs were reptiles, they must have looked very different from the reptiles that are living today.

All of today's reptiles are cold-blooded. A cold-blooded creature can move quickly for only a few minutes at a time. If it gets too cold, it moves very slowly and must warm itself in the sun before it can move quickly again. Since flying would be hard for a cold-blooded animal, many scientists now think pterosaurs were warm-blooded like human beings.

Some pterosaurs were covered with fur! When scientists thought that pterosaurs were reptiles, they assumed that the animals must have been covered with scaly reptile skin. But many other scientists thought pterosaurs would have needed fur or feathers to keep them warm as they flew.

The argument was finally settled in 1970 when a pterosaur fossil discovered in Russia clearly showed long fur. Since then other furry pterosaur fossils have been found and we can be sure that at least some pterosaurs were furry.

Everything we know about life in the age of dinosaurs has been learned from studying fossils. Fossils are made when a dead animal or plant is buried in mud or sand. Over millions of years, the mud turns to stone, leaving an imprint of the plant or animal.

Studying fossils can tell us much about the pterosaurs. Fossil bones of smaller creatures inside a pterosaur fossil can tell us what pterosaurs ate. Fossils of plants and animals found nearby can tell us what the world was like when they lived. But there are some things we cannot learn from fossils. For example, we will never know for sure what color pterosaurs were.

We can make some pretty good guesses, though. Since pterosaurs lived like birds do today, they may have been colored like birds.

Their fur could have been colored for camouflage. The pterosaurs that lived by the sea may have been colored very much like today's seabirds—white underneath so the fish wouldn't see them against the sky, and a darker color on top so that larger pterosaurs wouldn't spot them from above.

Other pterosaurs that lived inland may have been brightly colored to blend in with the plants and trees. One, the Pterodaustro (tare-uh-DAWS-trow), probably lived in marshes like flamingos do today. It strained water through the bristles in its mouth to catch the tiny shrimp and algae the water contained. Since the flamingo gets its color from the shrimp it eats, some scientists wonder if the shrimp-eating Pterodaustro might have been a bright flamingo pink.

Pterosaurs came in all sizes. The smallest known was the sparrow-sized Anurognathus (an-ur-o-NAY-thus). It probably ate insects like many tiny birds do today. The largest, Quetzalcoatlus (ket-zahl-ko-AHT-los), may have had wings that spread 75 feet wide—as wide a wingspan as a twin-engined airplane!

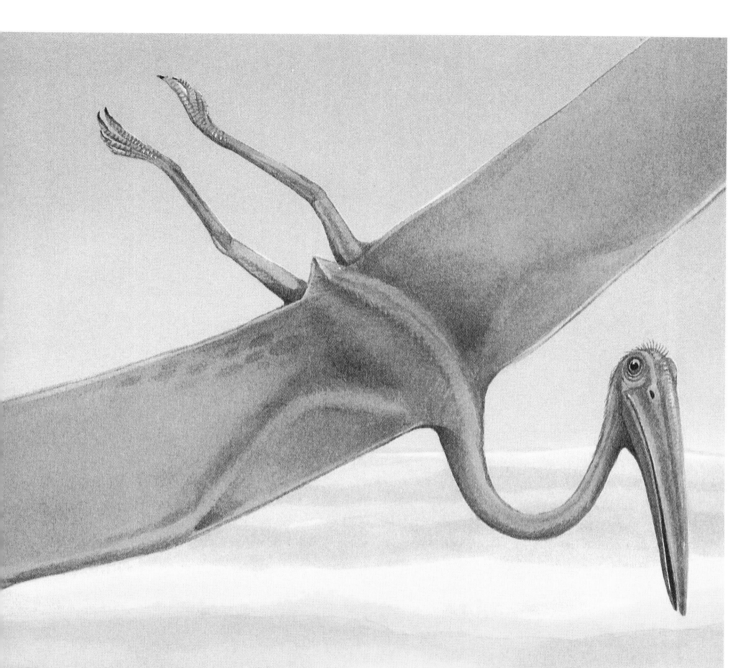

Pterosaur wings were made of tough skin stretched between the body and the wing bones. The bones in the wing were not all that different from the ones in our own arms, except that one finger was much longer than the others. It was this finger that gave the pterodactyl (tare-uh-DAK-til) its name, which means "wing finger." The bones were hollow like a bird's to make them light and strong.

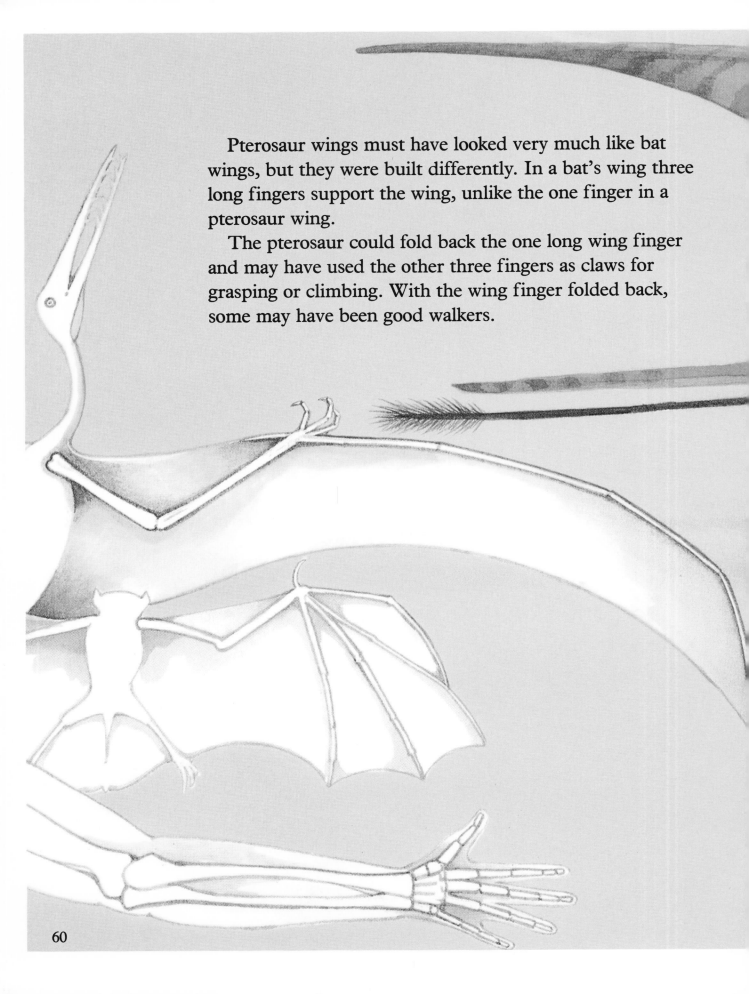

Pterosaur wings must have looked very much like bat wings, but they were built differently. In a bat's wing three long fingers support the wing, unlike the one finger in a pterosaur wing.

The pterosaur could fold back the one long wing finger and may have used the other three fingers as claws for grasping or climbing. With the wing finger folded back, some may have been good walkers.

When the pterodactyl was first discovered, it looked so strange that some scientists did not believe it could have flown. Some insisted it must have been a swimmer, using its wings the way a penguin does. Others thought it crept about using its front arms as legs and feeding on dead dinosaurs.

But now we are sure all pterosaurs could fly. A group of scientists and engineers recently managed to build a flying model of Quetzalcoatlus. The structure of the arm bones proves once and for all that Quetzalcoatlus could fly.

People often call any pterosaur a pterodactyl, but there were two kinds of pterosaurs: the rhamphorhynchids (ram-fo-RINK-ids) and pterodactylids (tare-uh-DAK-til-ids).

Rhamphorhynchids were the earliest pterosaurs. They were mostly small, and they had long tails that they must have used to steer and balance with while flying.

The little Rhamphorhynchus (ram-fo-RINK-us), from which all rhamphorhynchids get their name, had a diamond-shaped fin at the end of its long tail. It may have swooped down on fish and speared them with the long teeth that bristled from its mouth.

Another common rhamphorhynchid, Dimorphodon (di-MOR-fo-don), had an enormous head and a long tail. It may have lived in flocks by the ocean, feeding on fish and squid.

Later pterosaurs had no tails. These are called the pterodactylids, after Pterodactylus. Pterodactylids had huge heads, often with crests, which they may have used to steer with while flying. They were the biggest and the last of the pterosaurs.

Many pterosaurs nested like birds, in large colonies called rookeries. We know this from hundreds of fossils of tiny pterosaurs that have been found in one place. The mothers probably took care of the young after they hatched from the eggs. Some pterosaurs may have built single nests high up on cliffs and mountains, where the little pterosaurs would be safe from hungry animals.

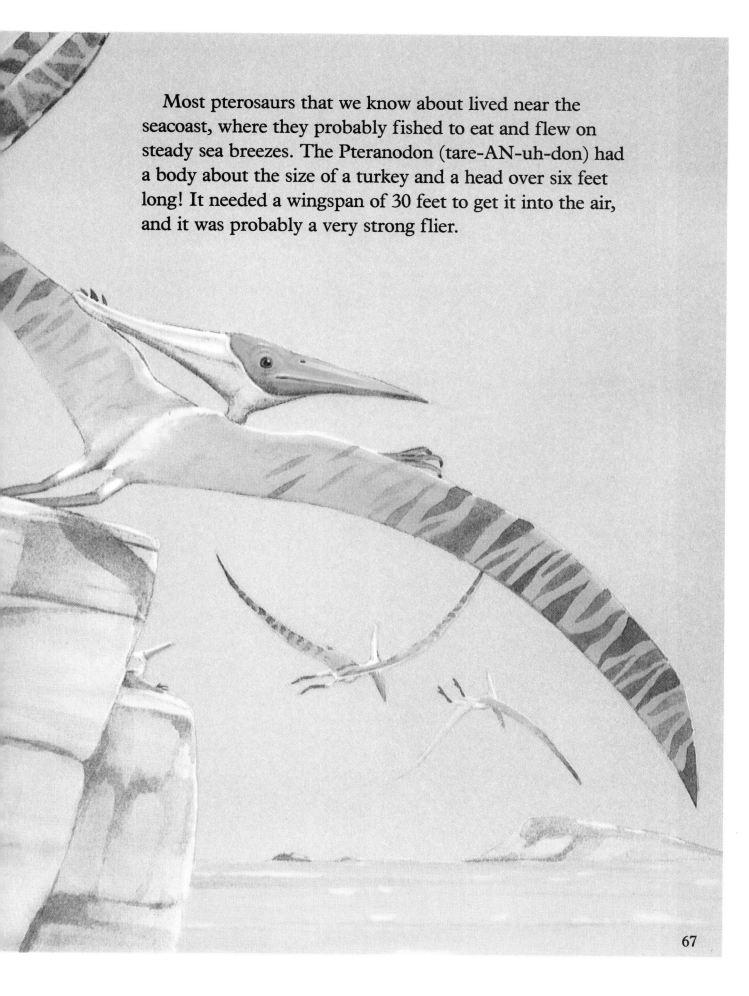

Most pterosaurs that we know about lived near the seacoast, where they probably fished to eat and flew on steady sea breezes. The Pteranodon (tare-AN-uh-don) had a body about the size of a turkey and a head over six feet long! It needed a wingspan of 30 feet to get it into the air, and it was probably a very strong flier.

The largest pterosaur known, the gigantic Quetzalcoatlus, lived far inland. No one has yet found a complete skeleton of a Quetzalcoatlus, but we do know that it had a long neck and a toothless beak like a bird's.

A big pterodactyl may not have been strong enough to
get airborne without help. Help could come from the wind,
or from a cliff from which to leap. Once a pterodactyl was
in the air, it would soar like a hang glider, letting the air
currents do most of the work. Since a grounded pterosaur
would have been easy prey for a hungry dinosaur, the larger
pterodactyls would have been very careful never to land
when there wasn't enough wind to take off again.

The great Quetzalcoatlus was not only the largest of the pterosaurs, it was the last of them. Sixty-five million years ago both pterosaurs and dinosaurs vanished from Earth. Scientists still cannot agree why. But imagine what it would be like to look up at the sky and see one of these pterosaurs soaring gracefully overhead!